Willy The Woolly Worm

Written by Joe Sinclair

Illustrated by Rosann Proffit Powell

ISBN: 1500816353
ISBN 13: 9781500816353
Library of Congress Control Number: 2014914541
CreateSpace Independent Publishing Platform
North Charleston, South Carolina

Other books by Joe Sinclair:

Children's Books
Lulu the Snow Goat
Queenie and Little Joe

Educational Books
The Marathon Called Educational Leadership
Two Worlds of Educational Leaders

Running Books
Putting Life on the Finish Line
Getting Older, Moving Smarter
Crazy Tales on the Running Trails

Claryce Sinclair—Contributor

For over thirty years, Claryce Sinclair had a very successful career as an elementary teacher in the North Carolina public schools. She holds an undergraduate degree from Elon University and a master's degree from the University of North Carolina–Greensboro. Her experience teaching small children was very valuable in providing input for this publication.

Dedication

This book is dedicated to the elementary-school teachers and administrators who provide leadership for excellence in education. Their hard work and sacrifice are greatly appreciated. A special appreciation is extended to my wife, Claryce, for her support and assistance.

Special thanks to Carla Leslie for her valuable assistance in preparing this book for publication.

Foreword

Dr. Joe Sinclair's legacy is enriched with his newest book about Willy the Woolly Worm. For nearly twenty years, I have known Dr. Sinclair as an educational leader with innovative ideas that inspire everyone he meets. As the years have passed, I have reached out to him numerous times for advice or guidance as I have faced educational crossroads at the local and state levels. His words have enlightened and reminded me to slow down, think logically, and value the worth of people. Dr. Sinclair's instinctive commitment to leadership has a simple message that motivates the best in people. When Dr. Sinclair talks about being a young boy, the son of a principal, he recalls knowing he was going to be an educator his entire life; he never considered doing anything else. As a result of his lifetime in education, he has served numerous roles, none more rewarding for us than his role of author.

In his most recent story, we are reminded that learning is exciting and, most importantly, fun. You will enjoy the simple story of five children learning together about a little creature, Willy, and his thoughts predicting winter. The teacher in this story is a mountain man who guides the children's curiosity through an exploration and discovery of woolly worms. I suspect we have all known a mountain man that inspired our love of learning.

Thank you, Dr. Sinclair, for your continued commitment to the learner in all of us.

Kimberly Simmons
North Carolina Educator Evaluation Consultant

Can a little creature that inches its way on the ground help predict whether winter is going to be mild or severe?

It was early fall. The leaves were beginning to change colors and the air was beginning to feel cool in the beautiful mountains of North Carolina.

One September Sunday, five cousins and their parents went on a family outing near the South Toe River. After having a picnic lunch of hotdogs and Smores, Sammy and Elijah asked their parents if they could go exploring in the woods.

Sammy's mom said, "Only if you take your older sister, Sarah, and your cousins, Selah and Lexie."

"Don't go past the park ranger's shed," called Elijah's mom. "Stay where we can see you."

"We will!" Elijah promised.
In this park was a park keeper, who was also a mountain man. His name was Bill.

Sammy's mom reminded the children that Mr. Bill was in the park. "Tell him hello if you see him," she added.

Elijah waved, and he and his cousins strolled happily up the winding path into the colorful forest.

Suddenly the children looked down and saw seven or eight small fuzzy worms. They had rings mostly of black with a little brown. They were crawling over and under the leaves and sticks. Sammy picked up the most playful creature and named it "Willy." As he crawled, the woolly worm tickled Sammy's hand and then curled up into a ball. The children laughed.

The leaves on the path ahead crackled, and the children looked up to see Mr. Bill strolling their way. Mr. Bill, the park keeper, was very knowledgeable about the woods and the animals and plants in them. He was a real mountain man.

"Look at this guy we found, Mr. Bill," Elijah said, holding up his finger with the wiggly worm.

Mr. Bill smiled at the group and came for a closer look.

"Ah! You've found a woolly worm," he said. "Very clever creatures. They can predict the weather."

"He's really a caterpillar," he explained. "They only come out during the day and are found during the fall months with different colors of brown or black bands each year."

"Why different colors?" Elijah asked, stroking Willy's fuzzy back.

"Well, usually the bands at the end of the woolly worm are black, and the ones in the middle are brown or orange. The more brown or orange, the milder the winter. The darker the bands, the worse the winter will be," Mr. Bill replied.

The children crowded around Willy to check his colors.

"Hmm, mostly black rings on his body," the mountain man noted. "That means Willy thinks it's going to be a cold winter, and we should get ready for snow, soon!"

"What about the others?" Sarah asked, pointing at the cluster of caterpillars.

The children and Mr. Bill crouched down to observe the other woolly worms slowly inching their way along the ground. They all agreed that the rest of the worms also had mostly black bands on their bodies.

Mr. Bill told the children that woolly worms are covered with short, stiff bristles of hair and are constantly looking for a place to hide under bark, inside logs, or near rocks.

"They have a special substance like antifreeze inside their bodies that keeps them alive during the cold winter," he explained.

"They have tiny eyes and feelers for moving about, see?" He held out the caterpillar inching along his finger for each of the children to examine closely. Elijah felt his eyes blurring as he squinted hard at the tiny worm's body. He saw many feelers on its body.
"They move around by touching and feeling," Mr. Bill added.

The mountain man explained that woolly worms are sometimes called "woolly bears" in other parts of the country. They like green, leafy plants to eat, and someday, they'll turn into beautiful moths.

"Ooo, really?" Sarah said.

"That's cool," Lexie added.

"What does the moth look like?" Selah asked.

Mr. Bill said, "The moth is small. Some have white and light brown wings. Others have more brown with white lines in their wings. They all have 3 sets of legs and antennae.

After hearing the story about the woolly worms from the mountain man, Elijah and Sammy said good-bye to their new friend, Willy, and put him back on the ground to crawl with his friends.

Willy was happy, and so were the children.

The cousins heard their parents calling them. It was time to go home. The children said good-bye to Mr. Bill and left their new friends, the woolly worms.

On Monday, Elijah, Sammy, Selah, Lexie, and Sarah were still thinking about what they'd learned from Mr. Bill. They returned to their schools glowing with excitement, and they told their teachers and friends about the amazing woolly worms and their ability to predict the weather.

All of their friends and teachers thought that was a pretty interesting story.

Since the children were excited, their teachers also decided that the other students would be interested in learning more about the woolly worm.

After doing their research with various books and computers, this is what the teachers shared with the children:

- The woolly worm has a legendary ability to predict winter weather.

- It hatches during warm weather from eggs laid by a female moth.

- The woolly worm is actually a caterpillar or the larvae of the Isabella tiger moth.

- It has thirteen segments, which correspond to the thirteen weeks of winter, and it also has three sets of legs.

- The darker the band, the harsher the winter will be.

- It protects itself by curling up into a ball and playing dead when picked up.

- Before settling for winter, it survives by eating plants.

- It searches for hibernating sites for the cold months under bark or inside cavities of rocks or logs.

- When spring arrives, the woolly worm spins a cocoon (pupa) and transforms inside it into a full-grown moth.

In a few weeks, the weather turned cold, and the snow began to fall, keeping the children inside where it was warm.

As it turned out, it was a bad winter, and Willy proved to be a great weather forecaster!

What an amazing, weather-predicting little creature!

Reflections

Growing up near the mountains of North Carolina, I have always been fascinated with the weather-predicting capabilities of the woolly worm. These little harmless creatures have always had the reputation of predicting the upcoming winter weather. In many parts of the country, the worm is also known as the woolly bear. These are found throughout the United States and parts of Canada.

Although there is much speculation as to the reliability of the weather predictions of the woolly worms, several woolly-worm experts have tracked its color patterns over many years. Some of these woolly-worm trackers indicate a very high reliability rate for accuracy.

Whether the reliability rate is actually high or low, the woolly worm always sparks much conversation and questions—especially with children.

Source: 1999 Old Farmer's Almanac

About the Author

Joe Sinclair is an author, educator, and athlete. He has published two outstanding children's books: *Lulu the Snow Goat* and *Queenie and Little Joe*. In the field of education, his publications include *The Marathon Called Educational Leadership* and *Two Worlds of Educational Leaders*.

In addition to these four publications, Joe's athletic success has resulted in three books— *Putting Life on the Finish Line*; *Getting Older, Moving Smarter*; and *Crazy Tales on the Running Trails*. His remarkable career as a marathon runner after the age of sixty-two is noteworthy: he has completed over two hundred marathons after reaching that age.

Dr. Sinclair holds a bachelor of science degree from Appalachian State University, two masters of science degrees from North Carolina A & T State University, an educational specialist degree from Western Carolina University, and a doctoral degree from the University of North Carolina–Greensboro.

Dr. Sinclair served as superintendent of schools in various North Carolina districts for more than twenty years and was selected North Carolina Superintendent of the Year by the North Carolina School Boards Association in 1992. His father and mother were career educators, and Joe has devoted his life to helping young people in the educational process.

He has devoted decades of service to education, serving in many roles during his outstanding educational career at the local, district, and regional levels, in addition to working at the community college and university levels of education.

He and his wife, Claryce, reside in Statesville, North Carolina.

FEATURED CHILDREN IN STORY: L-R SELAH SHREFFLER, ELIJAH SHREFFLER, SAMMY SINCLAIR, LEXIE SHREFFLER, AND SARAH SINCLAIR. THESE ARE THE GRANDCHILDREN OF JOE AND CLARYCE SINCLAIR. THE PHOTO WAS TAKEN IN 2016 ALONG THE BANKS OF THE SOUTH TOE RIVER IN NORTH CAROLINA.